Evincepub
Publishing

# Evincepub Publishing

Parijat Extension, Bilaspur, Chhattisgarh 495001
First Published by Evincepub Publishing 2020

ISBN: 978-93-90362-81-3

# A smile
# &
# the valley

roktaxoy

## UTTAM ADHIKARY

# About the Book

Through this collection of poems, the poet takes us on an adventure where he discovers an imaginary valley and then takes us on a journey through it. In this journey you will get the taste of love and romance, you will explore the undiscovered corners of an agonized heart, and you will see how the poet invades the world of agony with the help of poetry and resumes his journey.

The poet writes about the eternal love, the hurt, the healing and the undying hope in love. The book comprises four chapters- the doting, the aching, the healing, and the never-ending.

# Table of Contents

The doting      1

The aching      39

The healing      77

The never-ending      93

# The doting

Your smile illuminated a hidden valley

and I discovered the dreamland

that's how the magic began


//that magical smile

You didn't smile

to enchant me

I didn't intend

to fall in LOVE

but I was enchanted

and i'm in love


//it was destined

My notion

about heaven

was proved

to be wrong

after seeing you


//there can't be a heaven without you

Every time

I look at you

I get confused

between

heaven and you

I see the angels

being anxious

the moon

and the stars

being envious,

envious of your

beauty


// covetous universe

An unseen temple

became conspicuous

as I saw you

feelings are burning

like the wicks in diyas

your fragrance

is spreading alike the

burning incense sticks

and my heart is

so devoted to you

as if it has become its priest


//LOVE temple

I was fed

a cup of

philtre

by your

cryptic

smile

ironically

you are

still

unaware

of that


//you don't know

what your smile can carry

A dreamy galaxy

that I can see

each time

you glance at me

your tranquil eyes

take away

my serenity

and I get

galvanized

by your

angelic beauty


// a glance & the galaxy

Every time you    S

            M

          I

          L

            E  at me I cross a sea of agony

I have been dreaming about you since the day I saw you. I've never talked to you for real but I always talk to you in my dreams. every time you pass by me, a mysterious wave of emotions touches my heart and starts beating fast. you are so beautiful but your captivating smile makes you the most beautiful. I try to look at your eyes but as you come in front of me, my courage dies.


//the baffling feeling

Your smile

sowed the seeds

of LOVE in my heart

which was about

to become a desert


I saw your long and

black free hair

blowing in the air

it felt as if

clouds were floating

but abruptly

started melting

as you touched

my finger


now it's raining
each seed is becoming

a seedling


//seedlings in a desert

The eye contact lasted for about half a second only

but it seems that the moment would last forever

my mind and soul would always remember


//the indelible moment

People say that God is everywhere

but there is no time

and space where you are not there


// I see you everywhere at all hours

Loving you endlessly is not less than

any religious doctrine for me

it is as pure as

the Krishna devotee's love for him


//my soul is devoted to your soul

I saw you last night in my dreams

you were so furious at me

that I did burst into tears.

But amusingly I was smiling

after waking up


//nothing can dilute my love for you

any adversity you pour would be

immiscible with it

Round the clock

I envisage my life

spending with you

often the dreams

do not let me sleep

even if I get slept

you appear in the

dreams and I spend

my whole life with you

in the dreams too


// can't think of anything except you

The waterfall evokes

the enchanting beauty

of your heavenly body

I'm strolling

towards the waterfall

I can hear your name

in the soothing sound

wish you were here

holding your hand

we could amble together

turbulent water

slippery boulder

the path seems to be risky

but I want to touch it

with bravery, alike the way

you touched me


//you and the waterfall

It just feels romantic

when I hold your hand

even if we are in a dirty slum


*this is love magic*

she replied

Your eyes and the lips did intoxicate me

I've lost the home key

and the control over my destiny

I'm lost in a dreamy city

Sitting like a drunkard in the middle of an alley

It's raining heavily, hails hitting hard

Clothes getting wet but baby I'm very happy

I'm not drunk yet not sober enough

to drive my feelings safely

it may collide with you at any time


// I told her before my first kiss

Your L

I

P

S possess molecules of nectar

I want to taste them

every day before my day

begins and before I go to sleep

My body has a desire

for your body

My mind has the desire

to know everything

going through your mind

And my soul is desiring

to get unified with your soul

My mind body and soul

all three got amalgamated

as your lips

brushed my moist lips

I could feel the release of heat

owing to the formation of

nectar compounds as I placed

my tongue below yours

and started to slide around


// the aftertaste

Don't call me hot baby

I want to remain cool forever

cos I'm having your heart

and maintaining low temperature

is crucial

to keep it shielded and fresh


//jest after the kiss

I want to fly with you

to an undiscovered planet


you have not yet discovered

the heavenly province of the

planet hiding inside myself

_her witty reply

You are in my heart in my mind and in my soul

now I am longing for the eternal union

when the two bodies would become a unified whole

Baby,

the sun's temperature

doesn't go down

during the winter

and so is my love

at times

you may not be able

to feel the warmth

of my love

but that doesn't

mean that my love for

you went down

at times I may make

you cry by mistakes

but my love is infallible


//it's eternal

The moment your delicate fingers with polished nails and a stunning gold ring in the ring finger were touching my fingers, the moment we were drowning in each other's eyes, playing in the projector of my mind in UHD quality stored in my brain memory. soothing sound of breathing, luscious eyes, flavourful lips and the captivating smile bringing the spring of youth alike the tulips, magnolia, chionodoxa, and the camelia.

//missing you

Anyone except you

willing to enter

into my heart

will have to break

the door, I don't have

the key and breaking

the door is not going

to be so easy

In fact, it's unfeasible


//when she asked me to promise

that I would never leave her

"She is so beautiful that

even her shadow

looks stunning"


//when someone asked me

how beautiful she was

She smiled at me

I smiled at her

and the two souls

embraced each other


// soulmate

Pale yellow saree

light makeup, free hair

and the smiley face

she was coming with grace

I could see a cryptic world

hidden in her eyes

the entrance to which

got opened

as she glanced at me

and promptly

I found myself within it

as she smiled at me


//that divine experience

I saw the door to heaven in her eyes

And it opens when she smiles

It was her bewitching eyes

that knowingly fed me

LOVE POTION

ironically

she is still unaware of it


//love potion

The sun in one eye and the moon on the other

I replied when she asked me

"what can you see in my eyes?"

She: you are so cool

Me: you are so hot


She smiled

and I felt the heat

she radiated

unknowingly

Every poem

you taste

is

a fruit of

my organically

grown LOVE

# The aching

Everything went

against expectations

as if

the sun rose in the west

and set in the east

as if

the sun started rotating

around the earth

as if

milk has become black

all the stars and the moon

that I see every day is fake

and the color of rose is

no more red


//fall in spring

I thought that

the rainbow was romantic

but now I'm realizing

the fact that it was you

who actually made

it romantic

yesterday I saw a rainbow

it didn't seem to be

romantic at all

it was downhearted

you know why? cause

you were not there with me


// you and the dejected rainbow

Your silence kills
millions of dreams
but your smile
brings back life to all
and love forces me
again to fall

when you smile
i gain energy
to run an extra mile
when you become silent
wind of the dreamland
becomes violent

when you smile
budding dreams
get fully bloomed
when you become silent
the whole planet
seems to get gloomed

your silence
screams in my heart
so loudly
resulting in the
melting down of
clouds of agony
few drops fall

through my eyes
and the rest gets
vaporized

Your silence resembles the deadly nuclear weapons
which can destroy the dreamland just in a moment

In a sky

full of stars

and the full moon

I'm failing to

find its beauty

blooming flowers

look gloomy

once at which

I used to look

astonishingly


//beauty is

invaded by agony

I'm stuck
in a lonely island LOVE
in the middle of the sea LIFE

water level is rising very fast
I'm screaming for help
and trying hard to escape
don't know how to swim

I'm going to be the gobbet
of the hungry gigantic waves
and the island
would get drowned

but one day the water level
would go down
and the island would be
discernible again
I'm enjoying the spectacular view
of the rainbow from here
and enduring
the heat of burning dreams
without any fear

//island LOVE

The fire

ignited by your smile

is still flaming

in my heart

agony is raining

hopeless wind is gusting

but failing to put out

will my heart

get burnt out?

or first I will get burnt

into ashes?


//will you douse it?

It's been years since you left

but it feels as if there is no rain

for the last few decades


the whole valley

is turning into a desert

no water in the river LOVE,

has been completely dried up

now I'm wandering around like a

tramp and searching for an oasis


//every dream is awaiting a drop of your love

The nature

and I cried together

our tears flowed down

to the holy river LOVE

H
  E
    A
      R
        T

was weeping

soul

was sobbing

however

thunderstorm

was there

so

no one

could hear

Earlier it felt as if

you were on the moon

and I was on the earth

but now it feels as if

you have flown

to the mars and I'm still

waiting on the earth

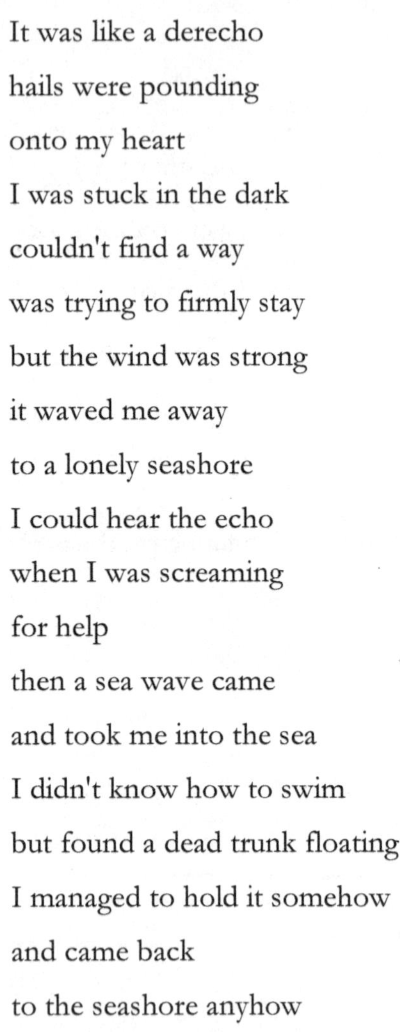

It was like a derecho

hails were pounding

onto my heart

I was stuck in the dark

couldn't find a way

was trying to firmly stay

but the wind was strong

it waved me away

to a lonely seashore

I could hear the echo

when I was screaming

for help

then a sea wave came

and took me into the sea

I didn't know how to swim

but found a dead trunk floating

I managed to hold it somehow

and came back

to the seashore anyhow


//the deadly derecho

The moment

you were gazing at me

raptly

that two seconds

your fingers were touching

my right hand's fingers

senselessly

often gets zoomed

and replays repeatedly

even at the dead of night

very clearly.


when the tremulous smile

appears

it gets paused

my lips start to move slowly

my eyes get closed

then I start kissing

at your cheeks very tenderly

When the mind comes back

to consciousness

I realize your physical absence

and see the dreams inside a

strong fence of unhappiness

each dream tries

to jump over the fence crazily

but they fail frequently


//hunting memories

The only door to enter

into your heart

where I used to knock

occasionally

is now missing

what I can see is a

seamless wall

long, tall and strong

seems to be indestructible

Feelings are burning

in my heart

Feels as if

I'm living in a desert.

Roaming around

like a nomad

and searching

for an oasis of love

baby i'm in thirst

of a drop of your love

There was a garden
of blooming dreams
in my heart
now the bloody despairs
are tearing them apart
but baby I'm not
going to give up

Earlier I used to miss you only

but now it feels as if

I'm missing myself too

I miss the old version of me

While climbing the mountains called LIFE

I had fallen down in LOVE

it was not gravitation

an angel was the force of attraction

since then the heart is broken

and I am living like a patient


alike a nurse a beautiful dream comes

holds my paralyzed mind's arms

takes me towards a window

and points me to see the rainbow


I see the angel flying in the sky

necklace is glittering, smile is sparkling

luscious lips are tugging off my lips

and I see living together our souls

and lives in her captivating eyes

suddenly I see her close to me

standing by the window

intimacy feelings have begun to flow.

my body is getting pulled

by her body

arms are moving to hold her hands

eyes are focused at her eyes

lips are ready to kiss

first the soft cheeks

then at the luscious red lips


the heavenly body smiles

winks, then flies away

and I fall down into the seashore


//how I fall for an angel

I'm missing

the alluring world

hidden in her eyes

the world full of dreams

where love would rain

birds would sing the songs

of joy and hope

the world where I used to

amble around with her

the world free from fear

the world free from despair

the world we lived together

//the world I miss

My soul wants to dive

deep into the sea

I saw in your eyes

for one more time

before it dies

I'm sorry

sorry for loving you

you weren't born for me

maybe I knew

but my heart didn't

it just loves you

I'm sorry

sorry for loving you.


you don't need to love me back

as someone inside me

tells not to even expect.

every dream is a pie in the sky

my brain can detect.


I don't know how to impress

I don't know how to love

what I truly know is I just love,

I just love you.

I'm sorry

sorry for loving you.


//sorry for loving you

And now the heaven I saw

in your eyes seems to be the hell

Are you hiding yourself here in the heaven?

Or flying to a different paradise

As I looked at her eyes

the clouds hiding the stars

started melting

I wiped out the first few

drops of the rain fell into

my eyes

then it started pouring heavily

I was drenched

and eventually I had to

run away when hails were

falling down in my head

I had to run away

under the roof of self-esteem

//time to move on

I'm trying to forget you
but I just forget to forget you
I'm sorry, sorry for loving you

My love is like the weeds

they grow even though you don't want so

they grow in my mind heart and in body also

you sprayed weedicides but they survived

you cut them often but they grow again

Feelings are flowing like a river

and I'm rowing my life upstream

away from her

Alike a flying knight the mind flies even in the darkness across the windy sky with its broken wings above many known and unknown nations searching your whereabouts. It stops flying when come across the river on the bank of which first time we got together. It lands there and shed tears after waiting lonely nights for a glimpse of your heavenly eyes.

Earlier I used to feel sorry for falling so deeply

Now feel sorry for not falling so deeply

He forgets to forget her

She tries but can't remember

_our story

Is this love or Pain in disguise?

Or Love is being wily and wise

Thousands of questions arise

To find the answers

I stay up day nights

But I fail and the soul cries

Love is drying up

and getting polluted

like some rivers

Melancholy is melting

like the glaciers

Depression is rising

like the sea level

in human lives

I'm a vagrant

roaming around

the cryptic city

POETRY


I used to live

in the edifice

DREAMY

erosion

by the river LOVE

rendered me here

The river of the valley has been dried up

The dreamland has turned into a desert

I've lost all the roads to escape

And probably going to get stuck and die in a

sand and dust storm

I wish my heart was hurt-proof

# The healing

Depression?

Close the door

of your room

Take a pen and

blank papers

Burst into tears

And write whatever

the hell you feel

without any fear


Is it still there?

Just repeat the above

whenever you feel so

You will see how

Beautiful your life is

When the depression

level is low

I've built my home

on the mountain MISERY

on the shore of LOVE

with my friend POETRY

Depression?

Turn the music ON

Play a sad song

Close the door

of your room

and

Weep

Wipe

Weep

Wipe

. . . . . . . . .

You will see the hope-light

I have bandaged my bruised heart with poetry
a day will come when while reading this
you will touch my bleeding heart's agony

No, you are not
Cause you have never
failed to love her
and more importantly
it's not a game
so never call yourself
as a loser or winner

my soul to me
when I considered myself
as a loser for the first time
on the day you got married

Agony is making my brain

more fertile

I've seen poems blooming

even in the day time

Don't cry looking down

when life becomes gloomy

look upward and

dance with the twinkling stars

No stars in the sky?

Enjoy the epic scene painted

by the clouds

Nothing is there?

Keep dancing in the darkness

until the sunshine reaches you


//sunshine is waiting to witness

your dance

Yesterday I cried

but I had enjoyed

the weeping

before sleeping

because of an

astonishing dream

dancing

in my tear-fall

alike the way

you danced

in the waterfall


// the beautiful poem
I saw in my tear-fall

Pain makes my pen more powerful

conveying the strength to fight with

depression

and eventually life becomes beautiful

when I see my bruised heart being artful

I don't know if I am a poet

but now I can harness

the sadness into happiness

I can make something

out of the pain which can

help it to restrain

The void created by you

in my heart

is now being filled up

by poetry's broken parts

Someone embraces me

when my heart screams

helplessly


I hear an angry voice saying

I am poetry I am poetry

when I ask

who are you my dreamy?


she appears dressing up

heavenly

cries in search of words

and awakens me midnight


wiping out tears of each other

we fight fearlessly with despair

and get committed to be together


I embrace her back

and she becomes my life-mate


//Poetry: my life mate

You're learning to cope with agony

you are on the way of self-discovery

I'm not less than any therapy

_poetry

Remember my dear

If there is polar night

then there will be polar

day also when the sun

never sets and you will

see the midnight sun

The collapsed dreamland is now reviving. abandoned seeds becoming seedling. dream buds are blooming, fragrance of which is spreading across the valley by sea breeze. the drowned temple of the island LOVE is now perceptible. rivers are flowing normally. I hear birds' chirping occasionally and can see the rainbow being smiley.

// the dreamland is reviving and the valley is smiling

# The Never-ending

I'm

wandering

around

in the river

LOVE

seating

in the boat

POETRY

rowing

by the oar

HOPE

Even in the

darkest night

the flighty mind

flies high

with its

broken wings

to touch the sky

You will come....

love will rain...

my dry heart will

get drenched

and the seeds of dream

will germinate again


you will come....

the moon will radiate

light of happiness

my dark life

will become flashy

and show me the path

to the right destiny


you will come....

my heart-wrenching

poetry will smile

and I shall be dancing

for a while

then I would start

loving the pain

and dance again

as happiness would rain


//you will come

Even today

the heart

craves for you

but now it's

under the radar

as I told

my heart that

now it can be

a crime

Not LOVE

My soul's craving for you is undying

Even if it dies it will rebirth like a phoenix

Which is beyond metaphysics or biophysics

You can go as far as you can

you can fly as high as possible

but my love will never die

anyhow the vapours of my

emotions will touch you in the sky

My love for you is like gravity

no matter how far or high

you through me away I will fall

I don't know if I will marry
but you will always be in my diary
you are the dream
my heart will always carry

Eyes are longing for a glimpse

of your beauty

ears are yearning to hear you

arms are craving to embrace you

fingers are yenning to touch you

my lips are itching to kiss you

baby my heart is dying to meet you


// the saudade

My love for you is like the universe

It's infinite and has no edge

In fact, it's expanding

And have no idea

when and how will it end

The wicks in the temple have been

extinguished and the whole valley

is moaning in darkness

but the wicks of love are still

flaming in my heart and the hope

is not dead yet, It's living

in the darkest corner with sadness

Even today I'm engulfed by the dreams I saw seven
years before and they look as beautiful as they were

Even today I get immersed in the sea I saw in your
eyes and it feels as beautiful as it felt seven years ago

Even today, my heart, the priest of the temple LOVE
is waiting opening the door for your arrival


//Baby the life may be ephemeral, not my love, it's
eternal